DUMBO

Copyright © 2014 Disney Enterprises, Inc. All rights reserved. Published by Disney Press, an imprint of Disney Book Group. No part of this book may be reproduced or transmitted in any form or by any means, electronic or mechanical, including photocopying, recording, or by any information storage and retrieval system, without written permission from the publisher.
For information address Disney Press, 1101 Flower Street, Glendale, California 91201.

This special edition was printed for Kohl's Department Stores, Inc. (for distribution on behalf of Kohl's Cares, LLC, its wholly owned subsidiary), by Disney Press, New York/Los Angeles.

Kohl's
1204205-00
123387
07/14–08/14

Printed in China
First Edition
1 3 5 7 9 10 8 6 4 2
ISBN 978-1-4847-2158-2
G615-7693-2-14182

For more Disney Press fun, visit www.disneybooks.com

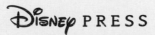

DISNEY PRESS

New York • Los Angeles

It was morning at the circus. Hopeful mothers looked up as storks flew overhead. Each stork carried a tiny bundle that held a baby animal.

Mrs. Jumbo sighed as she watched the happy mothers cuddling their babies. "Oh, dear. I did so hope there would be a bundle for me," she said sadly.

As the sun rose, the animals boarded the circus train. There would be another show the next day, and they had a long way to go to reach the next city.

The train had not been moving long when a stork landed on the roof. The stork dropped into Mrs. Jumbo's railway car. He had a large bundle for her!

Mrs. Jumbo carefully opened the bundle. Inside was a baby elephant.
"I'll call him Jumbo Junior," said Mrs. Jumbo.
"Look at him!" cried the other elephants excitedly. "Isn't he adorable?"

Just then, Mrs. Jumbo's baby sneezed. Out flapped two *enormous* ears!
The other elephants gasped. Then they began to giggle.
"He looks so funny," said one elephant. "Let's call him—Dumbo!"

Mrs. Jumbo didn't care what the other elephants thought. She loved her baby—big ears and all. She lifted him up in her trunk and gently rocked him to sleep.

The next morning, the circus parade made its way through the town. People clapped and cheered as clowns and animals marched down the street.

That night, the crowds hurried to the circus tent. They were eager to see all the animals.

"Look at his ears!" cried one noisy boy, pointing at Dumbo. "Aren't they the funniest things you ever saw?"

The boys laughed and teased Dumbo. Then one of them pulled the little elephant's ears.

Mrs. Jumbo trumpeted with anger. When she raised a hay bale to throw at the naughty boys, they ran away in terror.

"Down! Down!" cried the Ringmaster, cracking his whip.

The Ringmaster thought Mrs. Jumbo was dangerous, and he locked her in a small cage, far away from Dumbo.

Back in the tent, the other elephants gossiped about Dumbo's mother. "Such disgraceful behavior!" they said. "It's all *his* fault, you know." And they turned their backs on Dumbo.

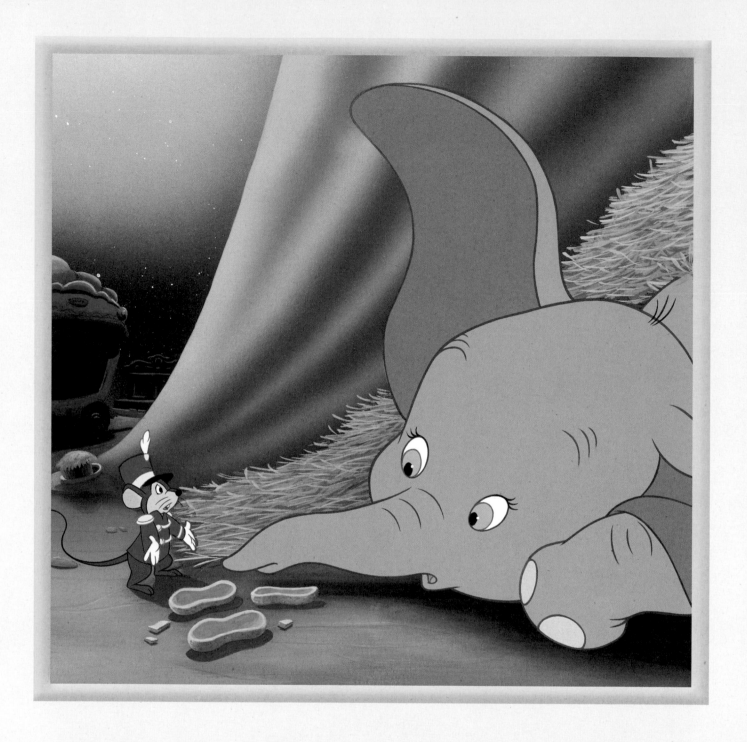

Nearby, a mouse called Timothy was watching. He felt sorry for the little elephant.

"All we have to do is build an act," Timothy told Dumbo. "Make you a star!"

Just then, they heard the Ringmaster talking in his tent. "I've got an idea!" he was saying. "We will make an enormous pyramid of elephants! All it needs is a *big* finish!"

As soon as the Ringmaster was asleep, Timothy crept into his tent. He scampered up to the Ringmaster's ear and said, "Your big finish is the little elephant with the big ears—Dumbo!"

"Dumbo . . . ," mumbled the Ringmaster, "Dumbo . . ."

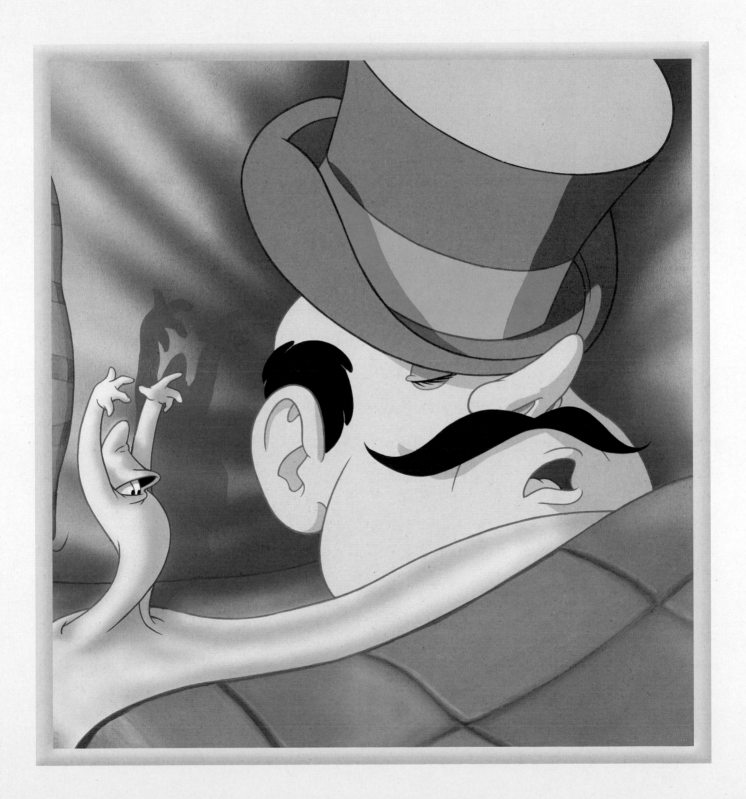

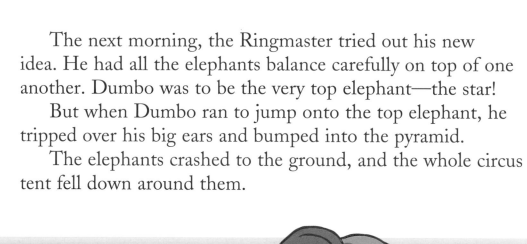

The next morning, the Ringmaster tried out his new idea. He had all the elephants balance carefully on top of one another. Dumbo was to be the very top elephant—the star!

But when Dumbo ran to jump onto the top elephant, he tripped over his big ears and bumped into the pyramid.

The elephants crashed to the ground, and the whole circus tent fell down around them.

Poor Dumbo was even sadder than before.

"We'll go and see your mother!" Timothy said to cheer him up.

Dumbo and his mother were overjoyed to see each other. Mrs. Jumbo put her trunk through the bars of her cage and cuddled her son, singing a lullaby.

All too soon it was time for Dumbo to go.

Sadly, he fell asleep and dreamed and dreamed. . . .

The next thing Dumbo and Timothy knew, it was morning.

When they opened their eyes, they found themselves high up on the branch of a tree!

The little elephant was so surprised that he lost his balance. Dumbo and Timothy tumbled down into a pond far below.

"I wonder how we got in that tree," said Timothy, shaking himself dry.

"Maybe you flew!" joked a passing crow.

"Yes, that's it!" cried Timothy. "Dumbo, you flew up there!"

The little elephant looked surprised. He couldn't really fly—could he?

"You just have to believe in yourself, Dumbo," said Timothy.

The crow gave Timothy an ordinary feather and whispered, "This is a
magic feather. It will help Dumbo fly!"
Holding the feather in his trunk, Dumbo stood at the edge of a cliff.
Before he could change his mind, the crow pushed him . . .

. . . and off he went!
All at once, Dumbo was flapping his big ears. *He was flying!*
"You did it!" cried Timothy.

That night, the Ringmaster put Dumbo in a new act—jumping from the top of a tall building onto a trampoline below.

Dumbo looked down. As long as he had his magic feather, he knew he could fly down safely.

Timothy was tucked inside Dumbo's hat. "Okay," he said. "Take off!"

But as the little elephant leaped into the air, he dropped the feather. He began to fall!

"Flap your ears!" Timothy cried. "You *can* fly! You *can*!"

Dumbo took a deep breath and began to flap his ears as fast as he could. Suddenly, he was flying! He didn't need that feather after all!

The Ringmaster was amazed! He watched Dumbo swoop over the cheering crowds.

The little elephant was a star!

Before long, Dumbo was famous all around the world. Crowds flocked to the circus to see "Dumbo, the Amazing Flying Elephant."

The Ringmaster released Dumbo's mother and gave her a special train car of her own.

And Dumbo and his mother were very happy.